CAN I KICK IT?

ISBN: 9781020001215 (Paperback)
ISBN: 9781020001222 (Ebook)

First Edition

10 9 8 7 6 5 4 3 2

45 Alternate Press, LLC
Hampton, Virginia
www.45alternate.com

CAN I KICK IT?

SNEAKER MICROFICTION AND POETRY

RAN WALKER

VAN G. GARRETT

CONTENTS

Foreword ix

Preface xi

1. Sauce 1
2. Limited Edition (Redux) 2
3. Sometimes I Stunt On Myself 3
4. Inferno 4
5. Tessa 1, Virgil 0 5
6. Stock 6
7. The Rumor 7
8. Tastes 8
9. Fly 9
10. Dennis 10
11. Uptowns 11
12. R.I.P. Jordan Debates 12
13. My Adidas 13
14. I'm Going Back to Cali 14
15. Fugazi City 15
16. Sneakers 16
17. The Hustle 17
18. Emancipation 18
19. Three Generations 19
20. Buddies 20
21. Can I Kick It? 21
22. Damn Fugazis 22
23. Eclipse 23
24. Dr. Dope 24
25. The Accidental Beaters 25
26. Grief 26
27. Feet 27
28. White 28
29. Bape Dreamz 29
30. Fila 30
31. The Class of 1987 31
32. Bethel High 32
33. Lucky 33

34. Slides   34
35. Doowutchyalike   35
36. Summertime   36
37. Go-Go Apples   37
38. Pigeons   38
39. Steph   39
40. Compliment   40
41. Astronaut   42
42. Hound   43
43. Sunshine   44
44. Puberty: II   45
45. Colorways   46
46. Outstanding   47
47. Loud   48
48. Snapshot   49
49. Crush   50
50. Daredevil   51
51. Flirt   52
52. Pastime   53
53. Song   54
54. Ex   55
55. Blues   56
56. Mythology   57
57. Hero   58
58. Money   59
59. Hip Hop   60
60. Dream   61
61. TQ: I   62
62. TQ: II   63
63. TQ: III   64
64. Lines   65
65. Exchange   66
66. DMV   67
67. Asics   68
68. Gangsta   69
69. Looney   70
70. School   71
71. Razzamatazz   72
72. Reseller   73
73. Seeds   74
74. Bookish   75

75. Oratory	76
76. Cartoons	77
77. 503	78
78. Simple	79
79. Waffles	80
80. Art	81
About the Authors	83
Also by Ran Walker	85
Also by Van G. Garrett	87

FOREWORD

During the most pivotal moments in my life, kicks have adorned my feet. My SB Dunks, scuffed glory from riding through Long Island and Harlem on a Chocolate board, stood atop the medallion in the foyer of the Schomburg Center for Research in Black Culture. A soon-to-be mentor asked me, "Do you know who is with you, in this moment?"

I didn't. I smiled.

He pointed to the doors in front of us that led to an auditorium. The title read, "The Langston Hughes Auditorium."

"Langston Hughes is with us in this moment, in spirit."

My mother read Langston to me in the womb; we recited the lines for "Mother to Son" while she cooked brown stew chicken, and I even garnered my rap name from "The Negro Speaks of Rivers."

He laughed, knowing my affinity for Langston. "He's also here, for real. His ashes are interred in the medallion you're standing on top of."

In this moment, I looked back down at my Dunks and welled up with emotion. The next time I remembered creating an almost identical snapshot in my mind, was on my first day in Ran Walker's classroom at Hampton University. He walked in, baseball cap in hand, denim jacket, kicks on his feet, with Junot Díaz in his palm, and told us to return the textbook we'd purchased from the bookstore.

"You won't need it for this class. We'll be doing something a little different." I looked at his kicks and then I looked back down at my Dunks, and I smiled. My professor wore kicks. My second Black male educator, in my lifetime, and the third father figure I would grow to adore…wore kicks, like me.

This was an affirmation. It was an affirmation that I belonged in spaces where I sometimes felt like an outcast. It was an affirmation that I was allowed to leave respectability politics in the spaces that forced them upon me. It was an affirmation that I could be me.

Crazy right? All that, from a sneaker.

That affirmation is what this book feels like. As a lyricist and sneaker connoisseur, I can affirm that Walker and Garrett have created a sidewalk. This book feels like solid ground—underground and mainstream kick lingo meet prose and moments sneakerheads swear only they have. It captures the feeling of capes, knowing that sometimes to be fly feels like flying, the excitement of a limited release that almost slipped through your fingers, the *woosah* of a close call on a swoosh, and the stomp of a kick that resounds in Mississippi clay.

The stories and poems in this book will manifest as a friend you've always known, one you can rely on to understand your love for soles and souls. You'll only want to ask it one question, upon arrival to its pages, "Can I kick it?"

Erica Buddington
CEO of Langston League,
HBO Def Poet, &
Bonafide Sneakerhead

PREFACE

I have always wanted to write a book about sneakers. I just didn't know how to do it. Last year I started writing microfiction (stories of less than 300 words). Using that particular form allowed me a lot of latitude to experiment with not just storytelling styles, but also the content I chose to write about. But I still hadn't reached a point where I saw how to clearly write a book about sneakers.

During a conversation with Mitchell Davis of BiblioLabs I mentioned that I was interested in putting together an anthology about sneakers. As I began to think about it, I realized the book might be more interesting if it were a flat-out collaboration between two people, much in the way that many sneaker companies collaborate with other designers. It was then that I knew who I had to ask to join me on this adventure.

Enter Van G. Garrett.

I've known Van since 2006, when we met and became friends on the first day of the Hurston-Wright Foundation's Writers Week. Over the years we've talked about everything from poetic forms to sneakers. In fact, during one of our more recent conversations, he mentioned that he had just completed his certificate in Sneaker Essentials from the Fashion Institute of Technology in New York. When I mentioned the idea for the book, he immediately signed on.

This book is the result of that collaboration. I have included forty microfiction stories, and Van has included forty poems. Of particular interest is the fact that Van, who writes a form of micro-poetry, elected to do something that he's never done before: writing succinct 25-word poems that evoke everything that sneakerheads love about kicks. Although the stories and poems are divided into two separate sections, the book, as a whole, looks at sneaker culture in eighty unique ways, parsing out everything that Van and I have come to appreciate about sneakers throughout the years. It is, therefore, my hope that you enjoy the stories and poems within.

So the next time you are hunting for that "grail" or reminiscing on a sneaker you copped years ago, savor those memories. They are stories, just like these.

Peace,

Ran Walker
June 15, 2020

For all the sneakerheads out there

I always wore sneakers when I wanted to. It was always about being comfortable and being myself.

— Whoopi Goldberg

PART 1

MICROFICTION

1

SAUCE

IT'S ALL my mother's fault. She's the one who encouraged Grandma Jo to find a hobby after Grandpa Steve passed away. Baking cookies. Golfing. Quilting. Crossword puzzles. Origami. Bingo. Scrapbooking. Really anything.

She had no idea Grandma Jo would become a sneakerhead. Now all my grandmother talks about are the latest pairs of Jordan 1 OGs she copped from some online sneaker raffle, and how all of her friends in the retirement community are now officially *dripped*.

Grandma Jo has also requested that, from here forward, our family refer to her only as Grandma Swagu, Queen of the Lace Swaps.

LIMITED EDITION (REDUX)

DeShawn had barely gotten three blocks from the sneaker boutique when the kid eased up on him.

"Run those kicks!" the kid said breathlessly, lifting his shirt just enough to show the glock in his waistband.

It didn't matter that DeShawn had waited in line for two days and had saved for months to buy them.

For a moment, he considered calling the kid's bluff, but he could still hear his mother's voice in the back of his head: "No shoe is worth your life."

So he stepped back slowly, placing the bag containing the shoe box at the feet of the kid, whose scuffed up Air Force 1s were probably stolen from another kid.

When DeShawn made it back to his house, empty-handed, he would remember the way he placed the shoes at the foot of the kid, like some kind of gift for an anointed king, a real Bruce Leroy punk-ass move that would take him longer to live down than the jacking itself.

3

SOMETIMES I STUNT ON MYSELF

THERE WERE several ironies about Jeff's sneaker collection. First, he only collected Nike SB Dunks, although he had never touched a skateboard in his entire life. Second, he bought only limited edition dunks, which he either won through raffle or paid massive prices to resellers for afterwards, which meant he could never wear his sneakers to the grocery store or even down the driveway to the mailbox.

He could only wear his sneakers at conventions, and it would take him weeks to select the perfect pair.

So in the meantime, he wore them across the soft carpet of his bedroom floor, eyeing himself in the mirror, posting shots for the 'Gram, and basically stunting on himself, to himself.

4
____

INFERNO

DANTE FOUND out that his sneaker boutique would be one of a handful of places in the world to carry the release of the exclusive Paris SB Dunks, the hottest shoe of 2002.

When word hit the streets, all hell broke loose.

People, including celebrities, called the store offering him money.

The sexy girl who worked as a barista across the street started sending him pictures of herself naked.

The guy who ran the pizza store next door offered him free slices for a year.

Dante was just relieved he would be able to get a pair in his own size. Outside of that, he couldn't be bothered with how the rest of the sneakers got distributed throughout the other circles of hell.

TESSA 1, VIRGIL 0

LITTLE TESSA HELD the tiny scissors in one hand and the black Nike swoosh in the other.

"See, Daddy!" Her eyes danced with happiness. "It was coming off, so I helped cut it all the way off."

He surveyed the room: the red zip tie slashed, the other swoosh lying on the floor, the attempts his daughter had made at wiping off the print on the side of the shoe with Coca-Cola (probably because she'd seen him get corrosion off a car battery using it). Those Off-Whites were *ruined*.

He started to yell, but he saw her angelic face looking up at him.

He ran over to her, tears in his eyes, and lifted her into the air, kissing her face as she giggled.

6

———

STOCK

JEFF'S FATHER didn't create a savings account for him when he was a baby. Instead, the old man copped hype sneakers and put them on ice, back before dead-stocking was a thing.

When Jeff graduated from high school, looking to head off to Ellison-Wright College in the fall, his father gave him a key for his graduation gift.

But it wasn't to a car.

It was to a controlled-climate storage unit packed with unopened sneaker boxes.

"You sell these, you'll have the money you need for school."

Jeff didn't believe his old man, until he set up an account online and started selling the sneakers.

The half million from the sale of the collection boggled his mind all the way through undergrad and deep into grad school.

He finally asked his pops what made the old man cop sneakers rather than stocks and bonds, like most parents.

"Never underestimate the value of something a man is willing to kill for," he responded.

Jeff was too afraid to ask what he meant.

7

———

THE RUMOR

JOEY HAD FINALLY SAVED up enough money cutting yards to buy a pair of Troop sneakers. He'd wanted a pair ever since he saw LL Cool J rocking them in *Right On* magazine.

When he finally got to school, the kids looked at him strangely.

They're just not up on this, he thought, but later that day his boy Eric pulled him aside.

"You know the Klan makes those, right?"

"What do you mean?" Joey asked.

"Troop means 'To Rule Over Other People.' Even LL doesn't fuck with them anymore."

Joey looked down at his shoes, suddenly feeling like the arrowed Troop logo was a swastika.

"I heard if you look under the insole you'll see the words 'Thank you, nigger, for buying our shoes.'"

Joey didn't look at that moment, but when he got home, he locked the door to his room and took off his shoes. He lifted the insole slowly.

They were completely blank.

He realized that it didn't matter, though. The kids at school still thought the writing was there.

He put the sneakers in the bottom of his closet, along with the copy of the magazine he'd carried around all summer.

8

———

TASTES

It SEEMED as if each edition of the new sneaker line was getting progressively uglier, as if it were in competition with itself to see how ugly a shoe it could make and still sell out on hype. It wasn't an experiment; it was a business model.

But the hypebeasts loved them and the resell value was strong, so he kept copping them, all the while realizing that sneakers were like music: your taste is set by the time you're thirty, and whatever comes after that is just noise.

9

FLY

ALVIN COULDN'T CARE LESS about the Louis Vuitton bag on her shoulder or diamonds on her wrists and fingers. It was all about the Jordan III OGs on her feet. The blue trim called to him like a siren on the high seas, her legs solid and firm, anchoring those beauties to the ground.

"Damn, that girl is fly as hell," Gary said, nudging his friend.

Unable to take his eyes off her sneakers, Alvin responded, "Yes indeed, my brother. Yes indeed."

10

DENNIS

DENNIS ROCKED bootleg Fila tracksuits his pops sent him from Seoul. It didn't matter, though, because they were dope. Plus, during 1987, we were brand-obsessed middle schoolers.

By the end of the year, we had all moved on from Fila, but Dennis continued to rock his now color-faded tracksuits. Occasionally he would show up to school in a new one, a different brand—also bootlegged—but it wasn't the same as the beginning of the year, nor was *he* the same.

11

UPTOWNS

Larry wore only white-on-white Air Force 1s, but he had laces for days, always swapping out colors and patterns, weaving them—flat, round, waxed, leather, fat, printed, or glow-in-the dark—in and out of eyelets and through an assortment of deubré to express his various moods.

What people failed to understand about Larry was that he was an artist. The shoe was his canvas, the laces his brush strokes, and the knot, if he chose to tie them, the brilliant bow that literally topped it off.

R.I.P. JORDAN DEBATES

THE INTERNET PUT an end to most of their debates:

The NBA didn't ban the Jordan 1. That was the Airship.

Jordan didn't even wear the high top Jordan 1. He wore mids.

Jordan had actually worn a different size sneaker on each foot.

Admittedly, the internet had taken much of the fun out of their Michael Jordan debates, had all but killed the apocryphal anecdotes that peppered their barbershop discussions, but they persevered on, exploring all of the rabbit holes of minutiae they could now discover. After all, what was a barbershop if there was nothing interesting to talk about?

MY ADIDAS

She couldn't have been standing more than ten feet away from him, killing it with the bamboo earrings and her hair pulled back into a bun. He wanted to step to her, ask her for her name, but the noise was overwhelming.

Then Jam Master Jay told everyone in The Garden to hold up their Adidas sneakers.

He slid out of his shell toes and held them up, along with everyone else in the crowd. He looked over at her, ducking around the raised arms and saw that she, too, was holding up a pair of Superstars, no laces.

Their eyes met across the crowded floor, and well —cliché, cliché, cliché....

14

I'M GOING BACK TO CALI

THE GUYS at the office thought it would be a funny gift, now that Frank was officially taking a management job out in the Los Angeles office, but what they didn't know was that he had every intention in rocking those high top Chuck Taylors every chance he got.

15

FUGAZI CITY

WORD on the street was that there was a kid selling Travis Scott Jordan 1 lows for $100 out of his house, so I went by to check it out.

A short kid with a dookie rope answered the door and took me to a temperature-controlled utility shed behind his house. It was filled with boxes of sneakers —serious heat. And, yes, he had the Travis Scotts.

I'm pretty up on my shoe game—had studied the "how to spot fakes" videos on YouTube—and couldn't see any flaws in the shoes. The price is what made me believe they had to be fakes.

But I couldn't be sure.

I didn't want to sponsor terrorist regimes and all that stuff, but I also didn't want to pass up a deal, especially if he had them joints in my size. Which he did.

As I carried the box home under my arm, I kept telling myself that I'd done the right thing. And by the time I got home, I almost believed it.

16

SNEAKERS

The argument began during recess, just before Mr. Bailey's history class.

The subject: Who invented sneakers?

Lamar and his buddies were on the side of Shuri, the princess of Wakanda, who made the shoes for her brother, T'Challa, when he became king.

Dexter Conroy claimed it was Wait Webster because his daddy had told him so, and his friends nodded in agreement, mainly because he occasionally let them cheat off of his quizzes.

Mr. Bailey put an end to the argument by telling them they were both right (he didn't know, but wanted to keep the peace).

Later that afternoon, when Mr. Bailey had a chance to decompress from the day and actually do a Google search, he laughed to himself, realizing he had actually told them the truth.

THE HUSTLE

By day, Lantrell worked the floor at a sneaker store in the mall, pushing shoe cleaner and water repellant, carrying boxes back and forth, looking at people's funky feet, all while listening to the same soundtrack looping on the stores speakers.

By night, he took the limited edition sneakers he'd stashed in the back and paid for with his employee discount and sold them online at a profit.

He made more from flipping shoes, but he needed the day job to make that work.

This is how Lantrell got through college—and he might have continued on like that, but he got hired by the marketing department of a large athletic shoe company. His job: building hype around limited releases.

Even though he had landed his dream job, he often wondered about the guy at the local sneaker chain, running the same hustle he had.

They were all cogs in the same industry machine, each having his own role to play, and, as a sneaker-head, Lantrell was quite all right with that.

18

EMANCIPATION

Clarissa's personal uniform included a white v-neck t-shirt, a pair of black skinny jeans, and a pair of black Vans Old Skools. She had a few zip-up sweatshirts, cardigans, and jackets, mainly in gray and black. The only bursts of color she owned were the assortment of silicone bracelets she collected every time she went to some type of convention or fair for her job.

"I don't see how you can wear the same thing every single day," her sister, Valerie, said. "I'm just too much of a slave to fashion to even begin to think like that."

Clarissa only smiled. She knew every element of her uniform had been painfully selected over the course of years, and while others continued to spend time obsessing over their clothing, she left herself plenty of time to focus on the other things that ful-filled her life.

THREE GENERATIONS

THREE GENERATIONS of men sat on the back deck beneath an outstretched awning, staring out into an August horizon.

Grandpa Allen said, apropos of nothing, "Back in my day you had to have Converse All-Stars if you wanted to be cool."

His son, Al, nodded. "I bet. When I came along, it was all about Jordans, especially the threes. Remember when I crushed all those cans and cut all those yards to buy them, Pops?"

Grandpa Allen smiled, nodding.

"What in the hell are those?" Al said, pointing at Trey's feet.

"Dad, these are Yeezy Boost 350 V2s. These are the latest hotness."

Grandpa Allen shrugged. "Don't see how you can play ball in those."

"Neither can I," Al added.

Trey smiled smuggly. "You don't ball in these shoes," he said. "You just look good in them."

Al cracked up laughing first, then the others joined in.

"I guess style just runs in the family," Grandpa Allen said, returning his gaze to the horizon.

20

BUDDIES

THE RED CLAY OF CARTHAGE, Mississippi, was unforgiving. In his youth, he had sacrificed plenty of white sneakers to the Red Monster, so when he sent his kids to stay with their great-grandmother for a week, he made sure to send them there with some black buddies—that way they could stomp the earth to their heart's content.

CAN I KICK IT?

Ever since the moment he first heard Q-Tip, Phife Dawg, Ali Shaheed Muhammad, and Jarobi, he was a die-hard A Tribe Called Quest fan.

Copped the red, black, and green Jordan 1s.

Copped every version of the Vans limited editions.

He longed to walk with the guys, to reminisce on their spectacular catalog, to speak to Phife in his Native Tongue, to just kick it—one more time.

DAMN FUGAZIS

Dear Mr. Anderson,

We have reviewed the Aira 5000 Elite LE shoes that you submitted to us for replacement, and our quality control team has determined that the shoes you sent to us were not manufactured by our company. Unfortunately, we will be unable to replace your shoes or offer you store credit.

In the future, we strongly encourage you to purchase our products from one of our authorized retailers or directly from us.

Thank you.

Maxwell Berry

Customer Service

23

ECLIPSE

ALICIA'S FATHER WAS A SNEAKERHEAD. She grew up watching him rock dope kicks, and by the time she entered high school, she found herself wanting to start her own collection.

"Make all A's this semester, and I'll get you your first pair of Jordan 1 OGs," he told her.

Not only did she get all A's over the next four years, she went on to graduate valedictorian of her class. By that time, though, her sneaker collection was on track to eclipse her father's.

DR. DOPE

THE STUDENTS widely regarded her as the dopest professor on campus. It wasn't because she always wore
the freshest kicks—although that part didn't hurt
either.

THE ACCIDENTAL BEATERS

IT WASN'T A FLEX: Earl wearing Yeezy Boost 380s to cut the yard in front of his house.

It didn't matter though. The hypebeasts in the neighborhood posted pics of him online, calling him bat-shit crazy.

What they didn't know is that he'd gotten them as a gift—had never even heard of the shoes before—and that he found them comfortable enough, to do yard work in anyway.

26

GRIEF

ON THE DATE of every Air Jordan IV retro release, the manager at the local Sneaker Kingdom would set aside a men's size 12 for Mrs. Sykes. He sold them to her using his employee discount. He knew she wasn't buying them for herself. Her son had been murdered for his J 4s four years ago, and, well, parents had different ways of coping with their grief.

FEET

HE HAD HAMMER TOES, bunions, corns, and a few of his toenails looked like petrified wood, but when he wore his kicks, he got only compliments on his feet.

28

WHITE

ALL OF THE kicks in his closet were dope because of the Black men who lent their likenesses to them, but he still couldn't understand why Black lives mattered.

BAPE DREAMZ

AT NIGHT he dreamed of stars in the sky, the sounds of the jungle rustling with life, as an ape sat bathing in the moonlight.

FILA

As TEENS, they obsessed over $300 velour Fila sweat-suits on some Boca Raton shit, back when the brand was based out of Italy and Björn Borg's racquet was still hot, back before Grant Hill played "Tender Love" on his piano for Tamia.

31

THE CLASS OF 1987

AT THE CLASS REUNION, he was no longer the funky fresh fella with the dookie chain and the British Knights, and she was no longer the fly sista with the Salt-N-Pepa haircut and the biker shorts. Still, when they looked at each other, both now grandparents, they saw only themselves as they once were: sexy motherfuckers who did that shit.

32

BETHEL HIGH

BUBBA CHUCK WOULD THROW touchdowns and pick off passes during football season and then dunk on and cross up defenses during basketball season. We knew he would be big. That's why we always rocked Reebok. He wasn't just their Answer; he was ours, too.

LUCKY

Lucky was known for wearing green suede "Clydes." Because he was one of the only guys on the block who rocked Pumas, we looked up to him. He said the green represented the dollar bills in his pocket.

Yep. They called him Lucky, but that might have been ironic. At least the Clydes they buried him in were fresh out the box.

34

SLIDES

Somewhere along the way, while Morris was steadily building his sneaker collection, he noticed a strange trend beginning to occur: there were a number of slides that cost more than actual sneakers.

They had apparently gone from shower shoes and flip flops to special molded and air-infused footwear.

Were you supposed to wear socks with them or be barefoot? Where exactly were you supposed to wear them?

He knew the athletic brands had answers for these questions, but he doubted they were willing to share them.

DOOWUTCHYALIKE

THERE WERE those sneakerheads who jumped over the athletic brands straight to the fashion brands, picking Louis Vuitton or Gucci or Prada or Bally over Nike or Adidas or Reebok or New Balance. Then there were the sneakerheads who only copped limited edition sneakers.

Teresa's collection was different, though. She collected general releases of regular everyday sneakers. She figured, given time, any shoe could become coveted, so why not just buy what you like?

SUMMERTIME

JEREMY COULDN'T REMEMBER *who* grilled *what* at the cookout or even how many people were there, but he *could* remember Chante Evans, whose smooth brown legs looked like a billion dollars against the crisp white of her K-Swiss.

37

GO-GO APPLES

STEVE JOBS never wore his socks up to his knees with a pair of baggy cargo shorts and an oversized t-shirt, so for that reason, and that reason only, many brothers in the DMV would not give him credit for wearing New Balance 991s.

38
———

PIGEONS

AFTER HOUSING HIS "PIGEON" SB Dunks in a glass case for fifteen years, Arturo was shocked when some neighborhood kid worked up the nerve to break into his apartment and steal them. He'd had them since March of 2005, and the previous owner had had them for all of three minutes before Arturo jacked them, so this was probably karma.

Maybe one day he'd get them back—but he knew, deep down, those days were now behind him.

STEPH

THE CHAINS of the net rattled with each perfectly arched shot Omar sank, as he imagined himself in a pair of Under Armour Curry 7s. He stepped back and sank another three. He knew that it was about the practice and not the shoes, but it didn't stop him from wanting to be one step closer to his idol.

40

COMPLIMENT

SHE WORE pumps at the office, but like many other women who worked in offices across the city, she went to work in kicks, her pumps pressed down deep into her tote bag.

Ignoring catcalls and zoning into the Anderson .Paak playing through her AirPods, she saw a guy leaning against a building smiling at her and pointing at her feet. She muted the music for a moment, curious.

"I see you in those Air Trainers," he said, nodding. "That's a dope look."

She nodded and turned her music back on. As she walked on to her office, she realized that was the first compliment a guy on the street had given her that actually made her smile.

PART 2

POETRY

ASTRONAUT

This must be what walking
In outer space feels like:
One slow foot
Before the other
A galaxy of stellar pride
Kicks bright as moonbeams

42

HOUND

I'm a keen beagle
Sniffing out a box
Of new feet treats
Drooling
Head wagging
Tongue out
Pawing
While unearthing leather
Mounds like fresh flowers

SUNSHINE

I'm not materialistic
I like what I like

Shoes are my thing
Not my everything

Just something that offers more
Reasons to smile every day

PUBERTY: II

In middle school
I wore a flattop
And high tops
Thumbed my nose
At shell toes
Nikes seemed to spite me
Converse did the trick

COLORWAYS

There was a time
When the colors of shoes
Weren't ultra bright
Didn't reflect
Like loud Easter suits
Or Skittles
Times changed for the better…

46

OUTSTANDING

I ran all the way home
Mud caked on white Reeboks
Heart pumping fast
Excited to tell my parents
I made an A in biology

LOUD

I had a pair of Converse
Bright yellow as banana slugs
Musty as onions
Cool as popsicles
Kick-flipping on a skateboard
When I was young

SNAPSHOT

I peeped some kicks
Zipping near the Houston Metro
Hot as jalapenos
Lit as a forest fire
Blazing a sidewalk
On a cool fall day

49

CRUSH

Briana had a lot of things
That I liked:
Her dimples and her smile
Her butt
The way her red Adidas
Popped like lip gloss

DAREDEVIL

I remember kicking up caliche
On a Huffy bike
Tan and brown with a desert scene
Landscaped someplace I've now
    forgotten
In my snug Roos

FLIRT

She stepped to me
Complimented my shoes—Basquiats
Also her favorite artist
We talked in the park
Shared hotdogs
Until the pigeons went to sleep

52

PASTIME

Monica loved soccer
But hated my Pumas

A freedom fighter
Who loved my Onitsuka Tigers

Green and yellow
Like the lush field
Where we picnicked

SONG

Tish in K-Swiss

Eva in Adidas

Brittany kicking Saucony

Teri kicking Nike

Toni rocking Pony

Maria rocking Fila

Alma in All-Stars

So fly rock stars

54

EX

I dated a woman
Who didn't care
For the flavor of my kicks
Liked the plain vanilla
Of boring dress shoes and
Expensive fancy ties

55

BLUES

Shoes can cost you
If you don't watch out

Shoes can kill you
You better watch out

Some people murder for shoes
Chasing after clout

MYTHOLOGY

Some people think
Black people only care about
Hairstyles and tennis shoes

That our dreams are basic
Self-serving narcissistic realities
Boxed and laced in *bullshit*

57

HERO

There are moments
When I feel like I'm jumping
From the baseline of a court
Two tongues hanging from kicks
About to save the day

MONEY

I thought my Folks' budget
Was as tight as shoestrings
Never undone to purchase
New shoe releases
I huffed
Wanted to be
Paul
Jason
Muff

HIP HOP

Run-DMC crushed
Walk This Way
Before I was old enough
To drive
Sporting laceless Adidas
And black tracksuits
On stages
Before they signed my shoes

DREAM

Remember Hakeem Olajuwon
One of the best Houston Rockets
And NBA players
Ever
Had a shoe—Etonic
Signed a pair for me
Facts
No lie

TQ: I

Honey colored skin
Rimmed frames
Legs that didn't stop
It was hard to focus
Words lodged in my throat
Looked down
Saw her Air Max

TQ: II

She was different
Took my soles
With her eyes
On Air Max Night
Laughed as if we had
Roamed and backpacked
The entire world forever

TQ: III

I'm usually more confident
Especially in my favorite shoes
But she hit different
The way her olive dress hit
Her curves
In all of the right places

64

***

LINES

There are neighborhoods
Where shoes hang from lines
Like ornaments on Christmas trees
Places where lives gone too soon
Are memorials in the watching skies

65

EXCHANGE

I got into trouble
In elementary school
Traded my shoes
With a kid who needed
A pair
We were friends
The rest of the year

DMV

I wanted to be Jay-Z
On tour
Stopped at the mall
Before a show
Got Classic Reeboks
White as milk
Every step a silent crunch

ASICS

I saw some Gel Lytes
For ladies
That made me think of
Grapes
Purple juice
Tangy bubble gum
And this cool librarian
Especially the librarian

GANGSTA

Listening to Ice Cube inspired me
To get some black Cortez's
Also known as G-Nikes
Wore them cocky to a track meet
To impress Kim

LOONEY

Mel pitched a fit for my Folks
To buy her the Space Jam shoes
White
Red
Green
Orange
Expensive and unlike anything
That we owned

SCHOOL

My students are so bright
Minds as sharp as knives
They cut to the essence of life
While wearing shoes I wish
I could afford

RAZZAMATAZZ

Some shoes are worthy of fanfare
Pomp and circumstance:
Heavy saxophones and trumpets
Blaring like on SNL
With dizzying energy
The right touches of jazz

RESELLER

I sized him up
Hoped his 11.5's were
Cactus Jacks in Oiler blue
Wanted to stop him
Before they were forked over
For a consignment

SEEDS

I always learn something
At farmers markets
Like how OAT Shoes
Can sprout flowers
Because they are biodegradable
In a field of beasts with cacti

BOOKISH

The librarian
In the pink and yellow Asics
Saw me trip
As I checked her out
Before I ironically checked out
A book about juggling

ORATORY

Have you ever been tongue-tied
Words knotted as you tried to
String a sentence together
As awkward as two left feet
In overpriced new shoes

CARTOONS

I was a kid again
When the Tom and Jerry Reeboks
Dropped
Jerry with a tongue stuck out
On soft detailed wheat leather

A standout

503

Remind me to get some
Patagonia kicks when I get to Portland
Green and mustard
To break in properly
Before a night on the town

78
___

SIMPLE

Do you know the feeling
Of sitting on a soft sofa
At the end of the day

Some shoes are like that
Perfect and Simple

WAFFLES

Do you know the real story
About how the Nike Waffles
Came about
In a batter of genius
That I hope to have
One day

ART

Some art is done on crisp canvases
Coming with toe boxes
And shoestrings attached
Masterpieces moving
And breathing beyond
Drab walls with little dated tags

ABOUT THE AUTHORS

Ran Walker is the author of twenty-one books. He is the winner of the 2019 Indie Author of the Year and 2019 BCALA Fiction Ebook Awards. He teaches creative writing at Hampton University and lives with his wife and daughter in Virginia. He can be reached via his website, www.ranwalker.com.

Van G. Garrett is a professor of African American Studies and Literature at the University of Houston. A graduate of the New York's Fashion Institute of Technology's Sneaker Essentials program, Van is an award-winning author whose work is appreciated around the world. His debut picture book, *Kicks* (Versify/HMH), is slated for fall 2022 publication. He can be reached at www.vanggarrettpoet.com.

ALSO BY VAN G. GARRETT

Songs in Blue Negritude

ZURI: Love Songs

The Iron Legs in the Trees

49: Wings & Prayers

Lennox in Twelve: Poems

HOG: Poems

Water Bodies: Poems

Pit Bulls and J-Walks